SATURDAY

My Favorite Day!

WRITTEN BY
TASHA MICHELLE

ILLUSTRATED BY
ABIRA DAS

SATURDAY MY FAVORITE DAY!

ISBN: 978-0-578-87025-0

Dedicated to Mom, Dad,
Grandma BM, and Grandma Ruby
who created magical Saturdays
over and over again!

IT's **SATURDAY!**
MY FAVORITE DAY
OF THE WEEK!

NO SCHOOL TODAY-JUST ME,
MOMMY AND DADDY DAY!

IT'S CARTOONS, CEREAL, AND MY FAVORITE BLANKET DAY!

WEARING MY FAVORITE SHIRT, PANTS, AND SHOES SO I CAN PLAY DAY!

IT'S A PART DOWN THE MIDDLE OF MY HAIR, WITH TWO AFRO PUFFS DAY!

HELP MOMMY WIPE OFF THE TABLES,
"DO YOU REMEMBA, SEPTEMBA?"
DAY!

SINGING IN THE BROOM STICK AND DUSTPAN HANDLE WITH DADDY DAY!

IT'S "GRANDMA'S HERE" DAY!

TURN UP THE MUSIC

SO WE CAN ALL

"BOOGIE WONDERLAND" DAY!

IT'S WASH MY HANDS AND HELP GRANDMA WITH DINNER DAY!

SET THE TABLE AND DON'T FORGET THE JUICE DAY!

IT'S MY TURN TO SAY THE DINNER PRAYER DAY!

ICE CREAM TRUCK COMING DOWN
THE STREET RIGHT ON TIME DAY!

IT'S "LAST ONE TO THE ICE CREAM TRUCK HAS STINKY FEET" DAY!

FRIENDS AND FAMILY ON THE PORCH,
WATCHING THE SUN SAY GOODBYE DAY!

IT'S WATCH A BUGS BUTT LIGHT UP
AND CATCH SOME IN A JAR DAY!

NIGHTTIME BUBBLE BATH WITH MY TOYS DAY!

IT'S JUMP ON THE BED AND RUN FROM
DADDY MONSTER IN MY FAVORITE PJS DAY!

TUCKED IN BY MOMMY'S TICKLE FINGERS DAY!

IT'S FAVORITE TEDDY AND BEDTIME STORIES WITH GRANDMA DAY!

HUGS, KISSES, AND SWEET DREAMS DAY!

IT'S SUNDAY!

MY OTHER FAVORITE DAY!

About the Author

Pittsburgh Native, Tasha Michelle, is a performing artist and children's programming visionary living in New York. She advocates for after-school programming and putting the arts back into public schools.

Tasha spends most of her time mentoring youth and young adults in the Performing Arts.

Website : www.BeanBagStories.com

About the Illustrator

Abira has been working as a freelance illustrator for children's books for authors from different countries and her books are available on Amazon and other online bookstores.

Abira calls Kolkata (India) her hometown and loves travelling when she is not working.

Website : www.artofabira.com
Instagram : artofabira

CPSIA information can be obtained
at www.ICGtesting.com
Printed in the USA
LVHW070930050921
697021LV00001B/4